Julian had a book from the library. By reading the book, he was learning to be a tracker and a guide and a scout. He had shown it to Gloria. He wouldn't show it to me.

"I could learn too," I said.

"You couldn't!" Julian said.

"I could too!" I said.

Julian shook his head. "A tracker is strong and silent. You're too little – and you talk all the time."

Huey is fed up with being treated like a little kid by his big brother Julian. This time he is going to do something about it. He is going to prove to Julian that he can be a tracker and a scout too. He can be strong and silent, and track raccoons and zebras, and even a tiger!

Huey's Tiger

ANN CAMERON
Illustrated by Lis Toft

YOUNG CORGI BOOKS

To Bill Cherry

HUEY'S TIGER
A YOUNG CORGI BOOK : 0 552 545775

First published in Great Britain by Victor Gollancz 1995
as part of *The Stories Huey Tells*

PRINTING HISTORY
Young Corgi edition published 1998

Set in 16/20pt Bembo Schoolbook
by Phoenix Typesetting, Ilkley, West Yorkshire.

Young Corgi Books are published by Transworld Publishers Ltd,
61–63 Uxbridge Road, Ealing, London W5 5SA,
in Australia by Transworld Publishers (Australia) Pty. Ltd,
15–25 Helles Avenue, Moorebank, NSW 2170,
and in New Zealand by Transworld Publishers (NZ) Ltd,
3 William Pickering Drive, Albany, Auckland.

Made and printed in Great Britain by
Mackays of Chatham plc, Chatham, Kent.

Contents

Tracks

Julian had a book from the library. By
reading the book, he was learning to
be a tracker and a guide and a scout.
He had shown it to Gloria. He
wouldn't show it to me.

"I could learn too," I said.

"You couldn't!" Julian said.

"I could too!" I said.

Julian shook his head. "A tracker is strong and silent. You're too little – and you talk all the time."

I hate it when Julian acts like that. It makes me want to fight him. But I didn't say one word. I just went away.

In the night I woke up and went downstairs. Julian's book was lying on the couch in the living room. I picked it up. I couldn't read it all, but I could see it was about tracks.

It had pictures of the hoof and paw prints of almost every kind of animal. It showed deer tracks and raccoon tracks, the tracks of zebras and giraffes and elephants.

I looked out of the living-room window. I could hear the wind. I could almost hear many animals outside. Very quietly I opened the front door and went out. I still had the book in my hand.

There was a full moon. I could see my own shadow on the grass, but I couldn't see any night animals. I looked for tracks, but there weren't any.

In real life I really had seen raccoon tracks once. I looked through Julian's book until I found some. I decided to

copy them. I found a sharp stick and went to where our drive divides our lawn in two parts. The drive isn't paved. It's pebbly and sandy.

Raccoon tracks look almost like human hands, with narrow fingers and long sharp claws for fingernails. I stood on the grass and used my stick to copy them along the edge of the drive.

I walked on the grass to the street. Then I walked on the paved street to the other side of our drive. I copied more raccoon tracks on that side – so it looked like the raccoon had gone back to the street.

I hid my drawing stick in the hedge and went back to the house. I was careful not to leave any footprints. I put Julian's book back on the couch, just the way he'd left it. I climbed the stairs, tiptoed past Mum and Dad's room, and went back to bed.

In the morning I went down to breakfast. Julian was running in the kitchen door with his book in his hand.

"Dad, Dad!" he shouted. "A raccoon was here last night!"

"Really?" my dad said. He went outside with Julian to study the tracks, and I went along.

Julian showed Dad his book. When Dad bent down to look at the tracks, I tried to look at Julian's book, too. But Julian wouldn't let me. Whenever I tried to, he covered it with his arm and poked me in the ribs with his elbow.

My dad stood up. "It sure does look like a raccoon was here!" he said. "Sometimes those little rascals come round to eat food out of rubbish bins. From now on, we'll need to keep the lids on tight."

The next night I woke up. I looked at the clock that sits on top of the brick on my night table. It was one a.m.

Julian was asleep with his pillow over his head. I went down to the living room.

I found his book on top of the TV, open to a page on African safaris. I went down to the basement and got my dad's hammer. I took it and the book outside. The moon was not quite as big as the night before, but there was plenty of light for working.

Every few feet I mashed up small spots of sandy ground with the hammer. Then I rounded them out just right.

I stood up and compared them to the picture in Julian's book. They looked the way they were supposed to – just

like zebra tracks. Zebras leave hoof
prints like horses. Their tracks are
deeper in the ground than raccoon
tracks. That's why I used the hammer.

In the morning, Julian was so excited
he was yelling.

"Mum and Dad!! Huey! Come and
look! There was a zebra here last
night!"

We all ran outside. My dad studied Julian's book and the tracks.

"Hard to believe," my dad said, "but it sure does look that way!"

"Could it have been a horse?" my mum asked.

"All the horses around here have shoes," my dad said. "These tracks don't show shoe prints."

Gloria came over and saw the tracks.

"Ama-a-a-zing!" she said.

She and Julian decided to make a zebra trap. They made the cage out of straight sticks tied together with rope. I brought them the rope from the cellar.

"We should put a carrot in the cage to attract the zebra," Gloria said. So Julian did.

He asked permission to sleep on the front porch, so he could watch for the zebra and catch it. Gloria got permission to stay the night and help.

Julian asked if I wanted to sleep downstairs with them to watch for the zebra.

"We could take turns watching and sleeping," he said.

I said there wasn't room for three of us on the porch. Besides I was tired.

But in the night I woke up. I looked out of the bedroom window. The moon was not as big or as bright as the night before. I went to the cellar and got a hammer, a chisel, and a flashlight. I crossed the living room on silent feet and peered out of the window to the porch.

Julian was on the floor in his sleeping-bag with his pillow over his head. Gloria was sitting up with her back against the wall, facing the zebra cage. But her head was tipped over on her shoulder. She was asleep.

On tiptoe I went out on the porch. The porch has one board that squeaks. I didn't step on it. The tracking book just touched Julian's hand. I put the hammer, the chisel and the flashlight under my left arm. I was scared I would drop them. I bent down. Very carefully, I reached out with my right hand. Very gently, I took the book. Julian and Gloria did not wake up.

I walked to the zebra cage. I set my tools down on the grass.

Carrots are one of my favourite foods. I picked up the carrot in the cage. I bit off half and ate it. I used the flashlight to check the rest of the carrot for tooth marks I had made on the other half. I worked on them with my fingernail to make them look bigger. Then, I put the flashlight down and put the carrot back in the trap.

I used the hammer to make more zebra tracks – into the trap and back out again. I checked them with the light from the flashlight. They were OK. When I finished, I found a fallen pine bough. I used it to brush out all my own tracks.

I went to the edge of the street. At the edge of the street there is a narrow, sandy place. There was room for some very good tracks. Elephant tracks!

Elephants are really heavy. Their tracks sink in. I used the chisel to soften up the ground before I made the tracks with my hammer. I made fat, round tracks, with bumps for the toe marks – five each on the front feet and three on the back, just like the picture in Julian's book. Afterwards, I shone the flashlight on them. They looked good.

* * *

"The zebra was here!" Gloria said in the morning. "He was here – but I fell asleep. Huey! You should have helped us watch for him!"

"I'm too little," I said. "I'm afraid of zebras."

Julian and Gloria took my mum and dad and me outside and showed us the tracks – and the marks in the carrot.

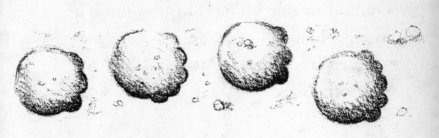

My dad studied the carrot. "Those are toothmarks all right," he said.

My mum took the carrot and examined it. "Some kind of toothmarks . . ." she said. "But —" She never finished what she was going to say, because Julian was shouting and pointing at the street.

"There're more tracks out here! HUGE ones!"

We all went running to see.

"They look big enough to be elephant tracks!" Gloria said.

My mum said, "What I don't understand is why all these animals are coming to our house. Do you have any ideas, Huey?"

Everybody looked at me. I had to say something.

"It's really strange!" I said.

I am a tracker and a scout. I am strong and I keep silent. I know many things. But I keep them to myself.

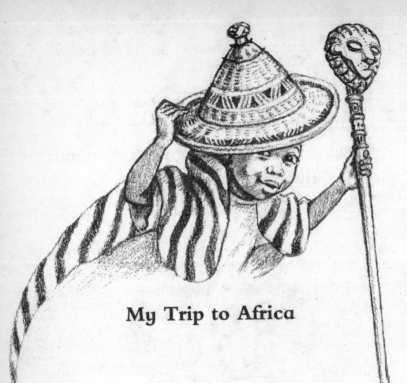

My Trip to Africa

I looked up. The sky was blue,
perfectly blue. I wanted to know why.

I went down to my dad's workshop
in the cellar. He was working on
Julian's bicycle.

"Why —?" I began.

"Can it wait a minute, Huey?" my
dad said. "I'm trying to figure this
thing out."

I went upstairs to the den. My mum
was sitting at the desk.

"Mum, why is the sky —?" I began.

"Oh, Huey!" my mum said. "I was
adding numbers in my head for income
tax, and now I have to start all over
again!" she said.

I went outside. Julian and Gloria
were kneeling on the lawn, working on
a new, improved zebra trap.

"Julian," I said, "why —?"

"Look at this!" Julian interrupted.
"We have the carrot partway under a
rock. A rope is partway under the rock

too. When the zebra picks up the carrot, he'll move the rock and loosen the rope. That will make the cage door fall shut and we'll catch him!"

"What if the zebra is too clever?" I asked.

"What do you know about zebras?" Julian asked.

"A real zebra would kick the cage to pieces!" I said.

I went back into the house and dived onto the couch. I didn't want to know about the sky any more.

It's not blue all the time, anyhow, I thought. Most of the time it isn't. So who cares?

I stared at the living-room wall. It had some interesting things on it – things from Africa my mum had hung up there – a straw hat from Ghana,

with green and yellow designs in it;
and a cloak from Mali with bright blue
and orange and white stripes; and a
walking-stick from we're not sure
exactly where, with the head of a lion
carved on it.

I kept staring at the things. The things kept staring back at me — especially the lion's head on the walking-stick. Pretty soon I realized something. I wanted to go to Africa. I wanted to see where the wild zebras are. If I lived in Africa, I would be happy.

I went into the kitchen and made three peanut butter sandwiches. I put them in a plastic bag and put the plastic bag in my rucksack. Then I went into the living room. I stood on a chair and got the hat, the cloak, and the walking-stick off their hooks.

I put the hat on my head. It was too big, so I put the cloak over my head first, and then the hat on top of it. That way, it fitted me just fine. I tried holding the walking-stick. It felt just right.

I went out of the door. I passed right by Julian and Gloria. They were working so hard on the trap that they didn't even see me.

I went down the street. The hat was good. It kept the sun out of my eyes. The cloak was good too. It felt warm. And the walking-stick was the best of all. It seemed to want to go places without me even moving it.

Once someone had carried it all over Africa. He had leaned on it when he was tired. He had used it to cross rivers. When he needed to, he had used it as a weapon. Right where my hand held it, it was smooth and shiny. The African hand that used to hold it had polished it for me. If I held on to it and didn't let go, it would show me the way to Africa.

I walked eight blocks. I got to the mall where the petrol station is. I know the man who works at the petrol station. His name is George. I asked him the way to Africa. He pointed.

"It's east of here," he said. "But be careful of the traffic."

I walked the way he pointed – towards where the sun was coming from.

I used my stick to climb the hill above the petrol station. I know the man who works on people's lawns up there. His name is Oscar. He was planting tulips.

"That's a nice stick you've got. Nice hat and cape too," Oscar said.

"Thank you," I said. "Do you happen to know the way to Africa?"

Oscar pointed.

"It's west of here," he said. He was pointing me right back where I came from!

"George at the petrol station just told me it's east," I said.

"You can get there going east too," Oscar agreed.

I kept going the way I had been going.

My legs were getting tired. I saw a woman sweeping her steps. I've seen her lots, but I don't know her name. She looks old and wise. She looked like she should know the way to Africa.

"It's south of here," she said. And she pointed. "South and east. Or, south and west. You could go north too – but that would mean crossing the polar ice cap."

"Everybody keeps telling me a different way to Africa!" I said. "Somebody is telling me lies!"

"No," the woman said. "No, they're not. Look!" she said, and she held her arms out in front of her, wide and curved.

"The world is round, like a ball," she said, "so there's more than one way to anywhere."

She drew paths in the air with her finger. She explained everything so well that I could imagine all the seas and mountains I would cross, and all the rounding I would do to get to Africa.

I thanked her.

"Good luck," she said. "The shortest way is about six thousand miles."

I turned south. My feet hurt a little, but I was happy. Because the whole world is connected. So even if it was a long way, I couldn't miss Africa. Even if I made a few mistakes, some day I would get there.

Big clouds formed in the sky. They looked like the walls and towers of the ancient palaces in Africa. They made me glad I was going there.

I got to the park where Julian and Gloria and I go sometimes. I went through the park to a big log we like to play on. I sat down.

Right in front of me was a tree. A dog stuck his head out from behind it and looked at me.

He was little and thin, with brown eyes and a tail that curved like a question mark. He had a cut on one of his ears.

I called him.

"Here, boy!" I said.

He perked up his ears as far as they would perk, but he didn't come closer.

"I won't hurt you," I said.

He sat down. He looked like he was wondering if he should believe me.

My rucksack was under my cloak. I

took it off and got out my sandwiches.
I held one out to the dog and said,
"Food, boy!" but he still wouldn't
come.

"I'll call you 'Tiger'," I told him.
"You're hungry – but you still won't
come just because a stranger calls you.

That's being clever."

He looked like he understood.

I put the sandwich on the ground half-way between us. Tiger walked up to it. He ate it in a gulp and stood and looked at me.

I finished my own sandwich.

"Do you want to go to Africa, Tiger?" I asked.

His body looked like he was saying no. His eyes looked like yes.

"Come on then," I said. I got up and started walking again. Tiger followed me, not too close behind.

It was beautiful and peaceful in the park. By the river lots of yellow flowers were growing. I decided to pick some for my mother. She couldn't help it that she couldn't add when someone talked to her. Probably only a genius could do that.

Then I remembered I was going to Africa. I couldn't take her any flowers if I was going to Africa. I sat down to think. I took out my last sandwich. I ate half and threw half to Tiger. He caught it in his mouth.

"We're going to Africa," I said. "But we don't need to go right away. We can go later. When we're older. When I have hiking boots."

I picked some of the flowers for my mother. I found a special stone to show my dad and Gloria. And Julian, maybe.

"Tiger," I asked, "do you want to come with me to my house?"

Tiger cocked his head as if he was deciding something. Then he followed me.

When we got close to home I could hear voices calling me. My mum's, my dad's, Julian's, Gloria's. In the distance I could hear Gloria's mum and dad too, calling "HUUU-EY! HUUU-EY!"

Tiger looked at me and sat down by the drive. I walked closer to the house. My mum had her back to me. She was shading her eyes from the sun and looking into the hedge.

"Come out, Huey!" she shouted. "This is not a joke!" She sounded worried.

I came up behind her.

45

"Here I am!" I said. I handed her
my flowers.

She didn't even look at them, she
just held them upside down with the
stems squeezed tight in her hands.

"Huey!" she said. "Where were you?
You know you're not supposed to go
anywhere unless you tell us first!"

"You were busy and Dad was busy,"
I said.

"We are never that busy!" my mum
said. "We need to know where you
are."

I saw my dad down the street. He
saw me and waved to Gloria and her
mum and dad. They all came running
up, out of breath and upset-looking.

"Huey!" my dad said. "Do you
know how long you were away?"

"I don't know," I said. "I was going
to Africa, but I decided I didn't need to
go right now. So I'm back."

"Huey," my dad said, "you must
never do this again. Most people are
nice, but some aren't. You could be in
a dangerous place and not know it. A
bad person could just reach out and
grab you and that could be the end of

you. No trip to Africa. Not even a trip home."

"I didn't go close to anyone," I said. "If anybody had tried to grab me, I could have run and screamed."

My dad stood over me and held me by the shoulders. "Next time you ask before you go somewhere!" he roared.

"Yes, sir!" I said.

Tiger barked. He was watching Dad and me. He had his two front feet on our lawn and his two back feet in the street. He looked like he was worried about what Dad would do to me.

"That's Tiger," I said. "He's my friend. I met him in the park and he came back with me. I don't think he has a home."

"And you want him to live with us?" my mum said.

"Yes," I said.

Everybody looked at Tiger. "He
looks abandoned," Gloria's dad said.
"Skinny. No collar."

"Can we keep him?" Julian said.

My mum and dad looked at each other.

"We'll have to call the animal shelter first," Mum said. "We have to make sure no-one has lost him."

"I'll call," I said.

Julian stayed out on the lawn with Tiger, so he wouldn't go away. The rest of us went into the house and I called. Nobody had lost a dog that looked like Tiger.

"If nobody turns up to claim him, you can keep him," Dad said. "But if you ever go off without telling us, he's going to the animal shelter. And he won't be coming back."

"I'll remember," I said. "I won't go anywhere without telling you."

So that's the way it was. We persuaded Tiger to come in the house and eat. And he stayed.

My mum put eggs in his food, and his coat got shiny. And now he trusts us. He's my dog and Julian's, and partly Gloria's too. But mostly, he's mine. I'm the one who found him. I'm the one who named him.

When I feel bad, I can tell him things I can't even tell Gloria. When I'm sad, he puts his head on my arm and licks my hand. He makes a little moan in his throat and shows by his eyes that he understands.

The cloak and the hat and the walking-stick are back on the wall. I'm glad they went on a trip with me. Things like to be used.

The world is a lot, lot bigger than I ever knew. And sometimes, I know, it can be dangerous. But it's beautiful, too. And some day I will go to Africa.

P.S.

Julian hadn't found any more tracks.
He really, really wanted to see a zebra
or an elephant. He got the idea that if
we had a tree-house, we could stay out
of sight and watch for wild animals
from above. So my dad helped us
make a cool tree-house in the pine tree
in front of the house. It has a big

platform, big enough for all of us –
Julian and me and Gloria – to lie on. It
has steps up the trunk that you can
climb to get to it. And it has a special
rope-ladder you can climb, too.

One day Julian worked out how to
get Tiger up there by putting him in a
basket that we hauled up with a rope
and a pulley. I think Tiger liked being
with us, even though he thought it was
a long way off the ground.

Once we got him up in the tree-
house, Julian started wondering.

"Maybe it's because of Tiger that
the animals don't come around any
more," he said. "Maybe they smell him
and are scared of him."

I wasn't going to say anything. I am
a tracker and a traveller and a scout. I
am silent. But I couldn't stand to be
silent any more.

"Julian," I said, "I was the raccoon,
I was the zebra. I was the elephant."
And I explained it all.
Julian got very angry.

"Why did you do that to me?" he said.

"Because of the way you treat me," I said. "You treat me like I'm little and can't do anything. I decided to show what I can do."

"It was a great trick!" Gloria said. "Huey isn't a little kid. And Julian, you deserved it."

Julian still looked angry. "You aren't a little kid," Julian said. "You're clever. But don't do that to me again!"

"If you don't treat me bad, I won't trick you," I said.

Since then, Julian and I have become friends. He even showed me everything in the tracking book, and read long parts to me – parts about the habits of animals, like how they like to come to water-holes at dusk.

The three of us read that together,
and it gave us the idea of making a
water-hole under the tree-house. We
put a big tub of water down there and
a smaller shallow one. We fill them
with fresh water every afternoon. Then

we go up into the tree-house to watch for animals.

So far some birds have come and taken big splashy baths in the shallow tub. Gloria's mum says if she helps out at home, Gloria can take some binoculars up to the tree-house, so we can see the birds even closer. My dad says he'll get us a book and an audio tape, so we can identify different kinds of birds – and get them to come to us by copying their songs. He said he met a man once who had studied birds his whole life. He knew how to call hundreds of different birds that way. He would just make one or two calls, and out of nowhere, dozens of birds would come flying to him. Maybe one day we can do it.

My dad says if anybody finds wild animals around here, it'll be us.

I think he's right.

BANANA SPAGHETTI
by Ann Cameron

"It's a new invention . . . banana spaghetti!"

Huey wants to surprise his mum on Mother's Day, so he invents banana spaghetti! It takes a bit of help from Dad to get it right, but Huey is determined to show everyone that he is just as clever as his big brother, Julian. And when Huey beats his fear of the dark, *and* copes with a dead fish, he proves he is as brave as Julian too.

Fans of the popular *Julian Stories* series will recognize Huey as Julian's irrepressible younger brother. Now Huey tells his own stories — featuring Julian, and their best friend Gloria — in this warm and humorous collection.

'Filled with ingenious details and written in a beguiling style' *Junior Bookshelf*

0 552 545767

IF YOU ENJOYED THIS BOOK, WHY NOT TRY ANOTHER YOUNG CORGI TITLE?

THE PRICES SHOWN BELOW WERE CORRECT AT THE TIME OF GOING TO PRESS.
HOWEVER TRANSWORLD PUBLISHERS RESERVE THE RIGHT TO SHOW NEW RETAIL
PRICES ON COVERS WHICH MAY DIFFER FROM THOSE PREVIOUSLY ADVERTISED IN
THE TEXT OR ELSEWHERE.

0 552 545767	**BANANA SPAGHETTI**	*Ann Cameron*	£3.50
0 552 528293	**HENRIETTA AND THE MAGIC TRICK**	*Stan Cullimore*	£2.50
0 552 529729	**BLOSSOM'S REVENGE**	*Adèle Geras*	£3.50
0 552 545554	**PICASSO PERKINS**	*Adèle Geras*	£3.50
0 552 528218	**ALL BECAUSE OF JACKSON**	*Dick King-Smith*	£2.99
0 552 527319	**THE GUARD DOG**	*Dick King-Smith*	£3.50
0 552 529796	**THE DAD LIBRARY**	*Dennis Whelehan*	£3.50

And also available, for older readers:

0 440 862744	**JULIAN, SECRET AGENT**	*Ann Cameron*	£2.99
0 440 863155	**JULIAN, DREAM DOCTOR**	*Ann Cameron*	£2.50
0 440 863333	**THE JULIAN STORIES**	*Ann Cameron*	£2.99

All Transworld titles are available by post from:

Book Service By Post, P.O. Box 29, Douglas, Isle of Man IM99 1BQ

Credit cards accepted. Please telephone 01624 675137,
fax 01624 670923, Internet http://www.bookpost.co.uk
or e-mail: bookshop@enterprise.net for details.

Free postage and packing in the UK. Overseas customers: allow
£1 per book (paperbacks) and £3 per book (hardbacks)